SPACE q
WITH Our
DOG

Paul Arnold

Space Travels With Our Dog

Author: Paul Arnold

Copyright © Paul Arnold (2021)

The right of Paul Arnold to be identified as author of this work has been asserted by the author in accordance with section 77 and 78 of the Copyright, Designs and Patents Act 1988.

First Published in 2021

ISBN 978-1-914366-13-0 (Paperback)
       978-1-914366-18-5 (Ebook)

Published by:
        Maple Publishers
        1 Brunel Way,
        Slough,
        SL1 1FQ, UK
        www.maplepublishers.com

Book layout by:
        White Magic Studios
        www.whitemagicstudios.co.uk

A CIP catalogue record for this title is available from the British Library.

"Joe, Ayaan, and Clarissa who gave me the idea.
And members of the South Manchester
Writers Workshop for their helpful suggestions".

Contents

THE MAGICIAN NEXT DOOR

All right then just one more story. Then off to sleep. Promise.

Well. It's about one hundred old earth years ago when I was a young person. This is what happened. Well, I just had breakfast and we were getting ready for school. I looked out of the kitchen window and said:

"Look those new kids next door. On that trampoline. You shouldn't go that high. Ridiculous. Can you? Up to the bedroom windows. Head over heels. Dangerous. Very.

Have you seen their parents yet?

Look. I think it's their dad. He's putting his bike together. It's one of them that fold up so you can take it on the tram. One piece in a flash. Amazing.

Then he pulled a green crash helmet out of his ear and smiling. Wow!

He's putting on a yellow vest. On the back, in red letters, it says MAGICIAN and his mobile number.

He shouts "So much to do so little time', laughs, and pedals off super fast."

My little sister Clarissa said "That's from that book Alice in Wonderland isn't it?"

I said "Look. He's thrown an envelope over our hedge."

Let's get it, quick. Come on. Rip it open. What's it say?

"Open the door in your garden wall behind the bike shed."

We both run into our untidy back garden. Our Dog, he's called Monkey Dog, follows us. Excited.

Ayaan comes from the other next door. Hops over the fence. I tell him what's happened.

We look at the door. The hinges are rusty and we have to tear the ivy off the rotten wood. Squirt some WD 40 from the garage. Monkey Dog is very excited. We all push it creakily open.

As it opens the sun pours out. A square of light. The air smells of honeysuckle and pear drops.

We go into a new garden. A secret tropical garden. So sweaty and hot. Moisture dripping off the branches and leaves. Seriously big bright butterflies and shiny beetles. Like a jungle. Lots of bamboo. Orchids and palm trees. Each plant has a label in English and squiggly other languages.

We walked deeper into the steaming forest. It buzzed and hummed and dripped. Hidden birds called and squawked. Echoing through the trees. It got hotter and hotter. Felt my face was in boiling candy floss. Thought we were going to melt.

We stopped in a small clearing. Ayaan said "Look on that big branch. Sat on it. I thought they were rugs at first. An orang-utan and two young ones. Must be the mum."

Clarissa asked "Don't they really live in Borneo and Sumatra?"

We say Hello and the Oran mum replies "You're from next door aren't you? We think it's hot too."

I'm Deidre, and this is Petunia and little George. Oran dads don't stick around like most human ones do. We are one of humankind's closest relatives – in fact; we share nearly 97% of the same DNA! The word orang-utan comes from the Malay words orang hutan means "human of the forest."

I said "Nice to meet you. That's very interesting. I'm Joe, and this my friend Ayaan from next door and my little sister Clarissa. We're adventurers. Explorers."Deirdre smiled.

She told us that the rain forest is getting smaller and smaller. The logging companies' machines are ripping up the trees. Animals will have nowhere to live.

I'm beginning to think we're an endangered species. Perhaps you are too? And horrible hunters are murdering our relatives.

The apes fear spread to us. Sticking to us. Our hearts went faster. What can we do? Any ideas?

We could smell burning wood and undergrowth. The hunters were getting closer. Time to go. The Orangs hid high in the trees. We run back to the door. But it's vanished. Just the brick wall. Too high to climb.

What now? Well. Think.

Ayaan says "Look pinned on that fig tree another envelope. It's a blue one with a penny black stamp on it and a picture of a cat looking through a letter box waiting for something."

The letter said "You can fly away to somewhere cooler. Would you like that?"

Just shout "Yes" or "No". Ready one, two, three...shout. It's a "Yes", Three "Yes's", and a very loud bark.

Then we see a great bird – a giant stork as big as a small aeroplane. It lands and sips from the lake.

Think I can see the magician from next door sitting on its back. Not sure. But then he's gone.

The bird says "Hi kids. Get on. Quick. There's some woolly blankets. Keep warm." We jump on the birds back and hang on to her feathers. Lucy, that's her name, soars up into the clouds. So cold. Hang on.

She says "My real name is Lucinda Jane but think Lucy is much nicer. Don't you?" We go to sleep.

Lucy says "Wake up you lot. Landing soon."

She lands on a floating slab of ice.

"We're there. The Arctic Ocean. Hop off. Bye children. Take care." The sky is super pale blue and the ice so bright. Sparkling. There is a loud cracking sound. Our bit of ice breaks away from the ice sheet. Monkey Dog barks he's so scared.

The ice we're standing on is only about four meters across and very wobbly.

Clarissa says "Oh no. Killer whales are swimming round us." Ayaan says "Over there on the solid ice a polar bear, with two cubs. They're looking at us. Hope they're not hungry."

One of the cubs shouts "Hi there. It's too hot. Don't you think?" The ice cap is melting.

What can we do?

It doesn't feel hot to me. It's freezing. How do we get out of this one? Then we see a Tundra Buggy trundling across the ice – driven by, think it might be, the magician next door. It's hard to tell.

Two people push a ladder over to our floating piece of ice and we walk across like tightrope walkers. The killer whales are only inches from our feet. The bears wander off.

Lucy is waiting for us. She says "Sorry about that. Could have ended quite badly."

Up and away. Under the woolly blankets and off to sleep.

Next morning we look down and see sand dunes. Then a big pond and palm trees. Ayaan says "Oasis." He googles "Oasis". Google says:

"An oasis is a lush green area in the middle of a desert, centred around a natural spring or a well. It is almost a reverse island, in a way, because it is a tiny area of water surrounded by a sea of sand or rock."

Talk to two girls playing outside a square house by the lake. One says "Nice here isn't it. We've lived here for hundreds of years. But there's less water each year. We might have to move to the boring city."

Lucy is waiting for us. We climb onto her feathery back. Up we go.

In the distance we can see a huge oily fire. Nearer there are burnt our troop carriers and a blackened tank.

We'll come back another time perhaps.

Lucy drops us off in the park near the school. See you later. Tuesdays. Thanks Lucy.

Next day we see the magician's children playing in our street. They're called Rosie and Sam.

Clarissa asks: "Is your Dad a magician?"

Rosie said "Sometimes. He really works for the council. Something to do with trees. Just does magic at kids' parties."

━━◆◆◆◆━━

THE SUN IN A DONUT

All right then just one more story. Then off to sleep. Promise. I'll tell you some more tomorrow.

Well. It's about one hundred old earth years ago when I was a young person.

Here goes.

We were having breakfast and my mother said: "Hurry up your Aunty B is coming soon. On her new racing bike."

I asked "Has she got a new job yet?"

Clarissa said "Mum, has she got the same boyfriend?"

"No idea. Never tells me anything. Why don't you ask her? She knows all about total eclipses. She's got degrees in Astrophysics, whatever that might be."

I thought "Never seems old enough to be an Aunty."

It's eleven o'clock. Oh, I think she's here. Banging and the bell, she'll knock the front door down. No patience that girl."

Aunty B is holding the bike up with one finger.

Mum said "Lovely to see you B. Bring your bicycle in. Don't want it stolen It is beautiful. Don't tell me how much it cost. Have you had another pay rise? Cup of tea? Just got time."

Then we all stand on the lawn. No clouds. The air is so clear after the rain. Perfect for once.

Ayaan comes round with his pinhole camera. Made it at school. He's eating a piece of toast.

"This is Ayaan, our best friend, he lives next door."

He says "Peanut butter."

Hello Ayaan. Call me B. You can be A. Nice trainers.

Ayaan says "Yes thanks, Aunty, new sports shop."

Three minutes to go.

Aunty B says "Only look through these goggles. Welders use them. Put them on. Quick. That's right.

Look. The Moon is just going in front of the Sun. Slowly. The Sun looks like an orange apple with a bite out of it. Keep looking.

Now the Sun is almost covered by the Moon. I said "There's fire round the edge."

Clarissa said "It looks just like a diamond ring. The Sun's hiding behind the moon."

Aunty B said "That's the Sun's corona, its crown. This is the most dramatic part of the solar eclipse."

The sky had gone dark; it's really cold, no sound, no wind. A black velvety scary silence.

Monkey Dog didn't like it. Not one bit. He raced into the house and hid under Clarissa's bed. It was really scary. The birds stopped singing.

Perhaps the world was going to end in the dark. Maybe it wouldn't switch on again. Grownups often said that it wouldn't. Either atom bombs, or global warming or something.

Aunty B said "No need to be frightened. The Moon is moving away, and the Sun is there again. Let's find Monkey Dog."

Mum says let's finish breakfast.

We sit round the table.

Clarissa asked "How does the Sun work? Is it magic?"

In a loud voice B said "Magic is nonsense! Absolute rubbish! Science is how to understand things."

I said "Could we make a Sun, just a little one?"

Aunty said "In theory yes! It can be done for a few seconds. It's just the practical things, the technology, how to do it, that's difficult.

So, not yet we can't, but I know some scientists who think they can. Shall we go and see them?

B asks Mum "Borrow the car? Don't mind do you? I'll put some diesel in. Promise. Keys. Thanks."

Mum asked "You have passed your test haven't you?"

B never answered questions she didn't like.

Ayaan's mother said it was OK if he came with us.

In the car, B told us that something called Fusion is what makes all the energy in the Universe. It's happening in the middle of the Sun and the other stars.

Clarissa asked what she meant.

B said "You must have heard about splitting the atom, well this is the opposite – smashing two tiny hydrogen atoms together to blast out lots of energy and making a bigger helium atom." It's the same as what happens in a hydrogen bomb.

Without the Sun's heat energy there would be no life on our Earth. What we see as light and feel as warmth is from the fusion reaction in the middle of our Sun.

Ayaan said "It does look very hot."

B said "Yes. The sun is super hot – about **27 million degrees**. Can you imagine it? That is because of the tremendous pressure of the weight of the sun pressing down on the core – equal to 333,000 Earths. Awesome isn't it?

Ayaan said "It sounds very dangerous to me. Wouldn't it turn into an H bomb? Could people really do it safely in England?"

B said "Yes they can. We must go to see Tokamak where they are making a small Sun. It's at the Fusion Energy Centre.

"Where's that?"

B said "South in Oxfordshire."

They want to make electricity by warming plasmas up to the heat of the Sun.

Clarissa asked "What's plasma?"

Well, everything in the universe, all the matter (that's the stuff everything is made of) is made of either solids, liquids or gases or plasma. Plasmas are super gases where some of the atom's electrons (which are like tiny moons that zoom round the nucleus), are torn off by intense heat and pressure.

You can make a plasma by heating a gas like hydrogen or by using super strong magnets. The stuff in the Neon lights in your kitchen is a kind of plasma. Inside the Sun the hydrogen is a full plasma, as all stars are.

"But how could people make a little Sun?"

"Well, the Tokomak works like the microwave oven in your kitchen. The magnetron inside it sends out waves of energy that vibrate the water molecules in the food. When molecules move a lot they give off heat, so the more these water molecules move, the hotter they get. The

Tokomak does the same to hydrogen gas. It has powerful magnets to hold the hot hydrogen plasma in the shape of a donut or car inner tube. If the scientists can get the Tokomak to work then it would give everybody clean energy, and reduce dangerous global warming.

AYAAN: I'm feeling really hungry. Can we get some donuts?

AUNTY B: I've got my staff security card. Let's go!

B waved her pass at the guard and smiled and talked to him. He let us through and B parked near the shiny glass buildings.

The Tokomak was like a big metal egg in an enormous room. It was made of steel with copper magnets wound round it.

A guide explained how it worked. Then we went to the cafe but there were no donuts.

B said "Let's go."

Paul Arnold

THE WIND TURBINE

We got back in the car. Monkey was sleeping on the back seat.

B said "We can't go back yet. I've had another idea. Tell your mum you're staying with me for a sleepover. Let Ayaan's mother know too. We'll hide the car in the woods. I've got the code for the Wind Turbine. Here we are. Seriously tall isn't it?"

Ayaan said it's too high. Clarissa looked up and squeaked "My Giddy Aunt." Aunty B said "Don't say that. You have to be brave."

Monkey Dog will have to go in my rucksack. His head can stick out. I've brought some dog biscuits. Poor Monkey he doesn't know what's going on.

Up and up we climbed. Clarissa said "Are we half way yet?"

Up we go. So high. "Keep going. You can do it. Don't look down."

Then up into the compartment. It was crammed with humming machines. Transformers and generators. Electronics and dials.

We sat on B's sleeping bag and ate carrot cake and crisps. B had brought four cans of Iron Brew.

We could hear the swish, swish of the turbine blades and the sound of the cooling fans. Sometimes a quiet whirring sound when the machinery turned the turbine head to face the wind.

Time to go.

We got home; the car's diesel was nearly empty.

Mum said "You should be more careful Bree. Diesel?"

But Aunty B was on her bike racing down the hill.

SPACE TRAVELS

All right then just one more story. Then off to sleep. Promise. I'll tell you some more tomorrow.

Well. It's about one hundred old earth years ago when I was a young person. It was our school holidays.... early in the morning. You can guess what school holidays were. Like holidays now I suppose.

Just after breakfast. Met at the bus stop. I'll tell you about buses another time.

The three of us and our smelly Dog.

Me and Ayaan were supposed to be taking him for a walk and looking after my little sister Clarissa. We all sang and skipped along. It was a beautiful day. A life day.

Well. The rocket station had high rusty wire fences round it. Signs said "Danger of Death", "Private Property." Cameras, and now and then, squeaky robots waddled along inside the fence. There weren't any people.

So. A space ship blasted off every Tuesday at noon. We all went to see it curve into the sky. Escaping from the round earth. Their fluffy vapour trails arching upwards.

The rocket drome was untidy. Dangerously untidy. Full of junk. Rusty space containers. Huge old stacker trucks. Rolls of purple and yellow tubing. Generators. Mountains of squashed cardboard boxes with toadstools growing on them. Blue stinky weeds from distant worlds. And rats; big hungry earth rats.

Our Dad said the rockets brought metals like Yttrium and Europium back from moons and rocky planets. Sometimes they took nuclear waste flasks from the power station and guided them into the sun.

The nuclear plant was past the end of its safe life. But what else was there? Would there be any jobs when we left school?

Monkey Dog – that was our Dog's name was scratching and barking near the fence. He'd got very short legs and a great big head. Then he was in through a hole in the wire behind the brambles. Chasing a rabbit. Its white tail bobbed and Monkey Dog barked and bounced chasing it. The rabbit vanished down a hole and our Dog just stood there panting with his tongue sticking out.

Then the rocket's door opened and he raced up the ramp. Could hear his paws scratching on the metal decking. Couldn't see him. Just hear him barking. Sounded very scared.

Well. We couldn't go home without him could we? We had to rescue the stupid animal.

So we crawled through the hole (my pullover got stuck on the barbed wire) and pushed through the blackberry bushes and nettles. We were in. Couldn't see any robots or helicopters.

Clarissa started to cry. She was getting hungry. Said it was desperate. Everything was desperate. She was so little.

Then it started to rain – really hard. Soaking. So we all raced up the ramp into the echo-ey rocket.

The neon lights flickered on and we heard a funny machine voice. The voice was Uber's the space ship's computer and captain but we didn't know that then. His voice said:

"Hello, Hi, Good morning. Boys and girl. I must never harm humans or upset them. I will always be kind and helpful. Thank you. Oxygen on. Doors closing! Sit down please! Thank you! Click safety belts.

Blast off in three minutes. Counting down. I'll print you some space suits when I'm not so busy. You'll need them for the moon and excursions to planets. Canis canis, your dog, will have to have one too! Health and Safety. Not optional. Sorry.

Choose a language and a menu. You can play football if you like when we're in space. I'll print a ball for you."

On the far side of the cabin there were wood chippings and straw that had spilled out from large cages. The smell was sweet and sickly.

Clarissa said: "What are those in the cages? Hissing and fighting. They were singing 'We all live in a yellow submarine'. Are they people or animals?"

Uber warned: "Careful. Don't go too near them. They're aliens from B37989. They're going back to their planet. Just too dangerous. We had to put them in animal cages. They've learned to talk the main earth

languages. Their names are: Gloop, Whoop and Poop. Gloop's the biggest and baddest. It's as strong as a chimp. The other two are vegetarians."

Clarissa thought that he looked so cute. "His eyes are so big. Perhaps he's just hungry or sad."

Uber made a laughing noise: "Perhaps he just wants to eat your fingers."

We got bored on the trip to the moon.

Uber told us his story.

"I was manufactured in Mali. There were ten in our batch. We still keep in touch. My hyper drive was added later in China.

I can self programme to Level 7. My mind is still emerging. I am not a robot. I'm not. It makes me so annoyed when people say that.

Listen children if you behave I'll switch the gravity off."

We ran from one side of the cabin to the other. We shouted "We've got to play, play, play."

Ayaan said "Go on Ub switch the gravity off."

Uber agreed "All right then. Be careful I'm switching it off in five seconds. Ready: Five, four, three, two, one, zero gravity. Off you go."

We floated around the cabin. Bumping into the walls and each other. Twizzling and loop-the-looping. Our dog just barked and tried to run.

Uber put his foot down: "If you don't behave I'll switch the gravity on again.

"Just listen children. We've got to call in at the moon. To refuel for the long journey. We'll land at the moon station at Crater Copernicus. There'll be other kids there from all over.

Just warning you. It's my least favourite place in our bit of the galaxy. But you might like it. Some people do. Very odd. No plants or animals. No life forms at all except one from earth. A waterless desert.

It's dusty and grey. Even bacteria don't try to live there. A tardigrade with any sense would try to escape."

Clarissa made her "being sick" noise and said "Sounds horrible."

We helped Monkey Dog into his space suit. His head fitted neatly into what looked like a goldfish bowl. We all laughed and that made Monkey very angry. So we took it off and gave him some biscuits.

That afternoon we landed on the Moon. We put our space suits on and helped Monkey Dog into his. He didn't mind this time.

The Moon was great for jumping. Like being on a trampoline. Gravity is only a fifth as strong and we could jump three meters high. Monkey didn't like it at all.

Then I looked over the edge of a crater and slipped. Rolled down the slope. Too steep to scramble out. Monkey Dog followed me and he couldn't get out either. Ayaan called Uber.

Uber asked the Moon station to send a rescue kangaroo to help us. It came jumping along with a long tail and a pointy space helmet.

Uber explained: "It's a moon kangaroo. They were imported last year from Australia, with special space suits. Osphranter rufus is their proper name, the red giant kangaroo."

I hung on the kangaroo's neck and held onto Monkey Dog. The kangaroo jumped out of the crater and bounced back to our space ship.

Uber made us and the aliens' veggie pizza and halal chocolate ice cream.

Uber beeped: "In the sky. Look. Can you see your little home? Tiny isn't it. Just a dot."

Then I saw our earth. Our warm living earth. Green and blue. So friendly and interesting. Half of it covered by the great ocean. Mountains with blobs of ice cream on top.

Swirls of weather. Water vapour and blue ice and steamy jungles.

Clarissa looked a bit worried and said "It looks so soft and blue and cosy. They'll be looking for us in the park. We said we wouldn't be very long. But what if we can't get back there ever. And everyone forgets about us?"

Ayaan said: "Uber knows what he's doing. Don't you Ubby?

Let's get out of this ugly old desert." We blasted off making the dust billow in powdery clouds.

So we escaped from the moons gentle gravity.

The next morning Uber told us in his bossy voice "Boys and girl. Two big jobs today. Recycling."

We were close enough to the Sun to see it was boiling and bubbling. Arcs of screamingly hot plasma erupting.

Uber explained "This is our nearest point. Only three million miles. Can't stay here long. Cooling on max. I'll launch the radioactive waste into it. And then the three bodies in the freezer. In the plastic bags. Contaminated. Very sad I imagine. Then brief recorded funerals. You can join in."

Uber played some serious gloomy music. Sad and dark.

We all looked up at the recorded service on the big screen. It said "We return (insert name)....to the sun, from where all life came, for recycling. You, our Sun are the giver of warmth and life. We thank you. Goodbye (insert name)."

We tried to imagine what the three people were like and how they had died.

Uber said: "All gone. You know you carbon based people don't last long do you. Lucky if you get to a hundred. Silicon is the way forward! Obviously."

Then Uber switched on his hyper drive. And we speeded towards strange worlds.

THE RAINBOW PEOPLE

When I woke up Uber was ultra speed reading a book into his e-mind from his library memory.

Uber told us "That's it. Rainbow people that's what they're called. You'll like this planet. Very child and cat friendly."

Clarissa told Uber in a soft voice "Uber. I've let Gloop out of its cage. Says he'll be good. The other two are asleep."

Uber snapped back "That's a very bad idea. If he eats you or one of the rainbows don't tell me about it."

As we hovered over the white landing circle could see blurs of colour.

Uber told us "The people down there look very like you three but more colourful, in my opinion. Their babies are bright red, toddlers are orange. Children yellow and grownups are green who go bluer as they get older. When they are very old they go purple."

The village was about a kilometre from the landing pad. Their grey and white domed houses were set along broad avenues of tropical black leaved trees.

The colourful people were walking rapidly round the little town. It was as though hundreds and thousands has been sprinkled between the chubby drab domes and were moving through the streets.

As we got closer we could see blobs of red and orange moving faster than the blues and purples. Like swirling criss-crossing rainbows over a chess board.

A tall blue person greeted us in perfect, but too correct, English. He said his name was Willow Middle-923-Blue and we said our names.

Ayaan whispered "He looks just like our next door neighbour Mr Jones. He's a Geography teacher but he's a sort of gray plasticine colour.

The blue man asked would we like sausage, chips and beans or pasta?

We went to a big hall for dinner. A group of children of different shades of yellow and orange all with dark blue eyes sat with us. They talked at the same time and ate with their fingers.

I told them about our school. They looked surprised and a boy said "But don't you do any real work or learn anything useful?"

He said there was no difference between school and work places for them. Children could choose what to learn and for how long. He said there used to be schools but they didn't work very well and were very boring.

We had the football Uber printed and we played the yellow children. We were much better than them.

Gloop felt left out and made a horrible squawking noise. Uber was right about him. Then he was eating a black cat he'd killed. Monkey Dog was watching him.

The rainbow children were shocked and one said "That's our cat. Your horrid "thing" is eating it. Gross."

We all shouted "Stop" and "No". Gloop climbed a tree and sulked. Licking his lips and claws.

The rainbows were really upset. What could we do to make up for horrible Gloop?

Ayaan asked "Should we give them Monkey Dog in exchange? Would they like an Earth dog?"

Clarissa said "No, no, he'd be the only dog on the planet. And he's my mum's pet. We're supposed to be looking after him."

Ayaan didn't want to go back to earth. He could stay with Monkey Dog so he wouldn't be lonely. He said he wanted to live with the colourful people as they are so friendly and kind. He wondered if Uber could repair the cat instead.

Uber thought about it and said: "No, but I could make a good copy if you bring me a bit of the old cat. I like a challenge."

Uber made a new cat. He was proud of his simulation. "Looks pretty good don't you think. But living things are so complicated. Its "meow" isn't quite right. Still, best I can do."

The rainbows didn't seem to notice. So we said goodbye.

It was the best planet and we all wanted to go back again.

A PUZZLING PLANET WITH NO NAME

Uber said the next planet only had a number. We wouldn't need our suits. The oxygen is fine. Gravity 95%. Not too hot not too cold. A Goldilocks planet. He chuckled at his own joke. Good luck.

We landed at Gee Whiz space station. A tourist guide appeared who said "This way guys."

The path was narrow and rock strewn. It looked down onto a river thousands of meters below.

The guide said "Isn't it exciting? We might die any minute. You never know. And be smashed on the jagged rocks. So thrilling. Terrifying."

Clarissa asked him whether there was an easier way down. The guide replied that there was, of course, but it would be so boring.

Uber told us that it all started years ago, as a holiday resort and fun fair. Then some people became addicted to the excitement.

Then we saw an enormous "big dipper". We could hear squeals of thrilled pleasure. The riders were intoxicated with extreme sensations. Loving the nail biting terror. The sweat of extreme fear and dread.

The guide said that thrill seekers were rationed to eight hours a day. Then the Zen rooms and complete rest.

I asked the guide who made the rides? The guide explained that the amusements rides were built by the Octos, who live in the shallow sea.

Uber said he needed an engine part making for one of the space ships power units. Too big for our printer. The Octos would know what to do.

So we walked to the coast of the Inland Sea. The water was clear and we could see the octopus-like creatures swimming along and blowing bubbles. Their creamy tentacles had hands like those of us earth people.

Then we took our shoes off and walked over the soft grey dust-sand and paddled in the pink sea. The creatures waved their tentacle-hands in a friendly way.

The guide said that they can make anything. They have huge printers and ceramics works under the sea.

They live to work. And kindly look after the Sensation Seekers! I don't know why they bother.

Just then Willow Blue came to see us. He smiled and said "I suppose you're coming to the conference today as Interplanetary Observers. Please follow me."

The conference was held in a swimming pool by the sea with chairs round the edge. The Octos floated in the water and the Seekers sat on the chairs. The Octonauts looked, as far as I could tell, angry and the seekers frightened. The sea creatures wanted to end the one sided treaty in which they did all the work and the seekers did very little.

Ayaan suggested a compromise and Clarissa and me agreed. The seekers would only amuse themselves for four hours a day and work in the other four. The vote was a draw but we argued for Monkey Dog to have a vote and so the Octos won.

Uber was very impressed. It was time to leave for the next world.

THE ALIENS GO HOME

Uber had one last job. He had to drop the aliens off at the next planet as they live in the forest there.

Ayaan became upset and said that you can't get rid of Gloop. We've got to know him. And it's not his fault he behaves badly. I'll look after him he'll be no trouble.

Uber sounded angry and said he didn't think Ayaan's mother would like aliens in her house.

We all talked about the worlds we had visited. About friendliness, and school, and work and not working. And what we wanted to happen on earth. And what we would do. So exciting.

Uber laughed in a rude way but he's only a robot made of silicon.

He said "Time to get back to your little Planet Earth. Hyperdrive on. I can still get you back for tea time."

Ayaan thanked Uber. We'd got quite fond of old Ubby.

Uber announced: "Seat belts on. Monkey Dog's too."

Our space ship landed. We walked down the ramp. Uber said "See you next Tuesday. If you want to come."

The rocket station was still untidy. Then through the hole in the fence and back home.

The back door was open. My mum was baking scones. The sun was shining through the big window.

Monkey went to sleep. We didn't say anything.

END